1st Ed.

Illust,

Garth Williams

#10.50

I

11.00

2.

D1283812

IN OUR TOWN

In Our Town

BY

DAMON RUNYON

Illustrations by
GARTH WILLIAMS

New York

CREATIVE AGE PRESS

CONTENTS

IN OUR TOWN

Our Old Man

Our old man used to have a motto that he had printed out himself in big letters pasted on the wall of his bedroom. It read: NEVER BLAME THE BOOSTER FOR WHAT THE SUCKER DOES. It was one of his favorite sayings, too.

He said it meant that you should never hold a fellow responsible for the consequences of an effort to do you a nice turn. He said many of his own troubles in life had come from getting the blame from friends he was only trying to help, like the time he took the stranger to a poker room back in our old home town of Pueblo.

The poker room was run by one of our old man's closest pals, a fellow they called Poker Joe. The stranger got to talking to our old man down at the Union Depot and wanted to know if there was a poker room in town. He said he was not much of a poker player, but that he wanted to kill a few hours between trains.

Our old man told the stranger he would be glad to take him to one of the nicest poker rooms he ever saw in his life. He personally vouched for the honesty and integrity of Poker Joe's. So he took the stranger there, and when the stranger pulled out a

3

roll of money that would have choked four horses, Poker Joe was so grateful to our old man that he wanted to kiss him. It was not often that a stranger with a big roll came Poker Joe's way.

Well, the stranger won all the money in the house in such a short time that he still had to wait an hour at the depot, and Poker Joe hit our old man in the eye with his fist. He blamed our old man for bringing the stranger in, and that was when our old man went to the *Chieftain* office and printed his motto: NEVER BLAME THE BOOSTER FOR WHAT THE SUCKER DOES. We sent Poker Joe the first copy.

Another time, our old man met a woman who was looking for a boardinghouse. He knew a fine place kept by a fellow and his wife who were great friends of his. Our old man was anxious to see these friends do well.

He took the woman to the boardinghouse, and she proved such a good client that the fellow and his wife never seemed to get tired of thanking our old man for doing them the favor of bringing her there. Then one day the boarder ran off with the husband, and the wife went to the *Chieftain* office where our old man was busy setting type and gave him an awful bawling out.

She called him names nobody suspected she ever

knew. She put all the blame on him for her husband skipping out, just because our old man had taken the woman to the boardinghouse. He sent the wife a copy of his motto: NEVER BLAME THE BOOSTER FOR WHAT THE SUCKER DOES.

Our old man said one of the worst enemies he had back in our old home town was a chap named Sam, to whom he introduced a girl Sam eventually married. Our old man had often mentioned to Sam what a nice girl this girl was, and finally Sam insisted on meeting her. He even thanked our old man warmly for arranging the introduction, but, of course, that was before they were married.

Our old man said every time he met Sam after the marriage Sam would recall that our old man had told him she was a nice girl. He seemed to feel that but for his recommendation he would never have married her. Our old man said personally he continued to think she was a nice girl, but he was not so sure of Sam's niceness, only he never mentioned that thought out loud, as Sam was a touchy fellow.

However, he sent Sam a copy of his motto: NEVER BLAME THE BOOSTER FOR WHAT THE SUCKER DOES. He also sent one to Mrs. Sam, but he said he doubted that she knew what it meant. He said he was afraid she might also be blaming him for the marriage.

Our old man said he guessed he had sent nearly everybody in town a copy of his motto. He said he never failed to send one to merchants to whom he introduced customers and who blamed him if the customers failed to meet their bills.

He said one time he sent out several thousand in the course of a single week on postal cards. That was the time a candidate for public office got him to go around town plugging his candidacy. Our old man told the voters that this candidate was a wonderful man for the job, and apparently most people agreed with him, as the candidate was elected by a considerable majority.

He immediately became one of the worst office-holders our old home town had ever known, and then a lot of people began remembering our old man's work on behalf of the fellow, and started blaming him. So our old man just sat down and sent those postal cards to everybody he figured must have voted for the officeholder.

Our old man once bought a hundred dollars' worth of gold mining stock from a friend of his named Chris, who said the stock was as good as wheat in the bin. Chris left town, and our old man learned that the stock was phony and was going to have Chris arrested.

Chris must have heard of the threat, and he sent

our old man a letter that kept him at liberty, because all he put in the letter was our old man's motto: NEVER BLAME THE BOOSTER FOR WHAT THE SUCKER DOES.

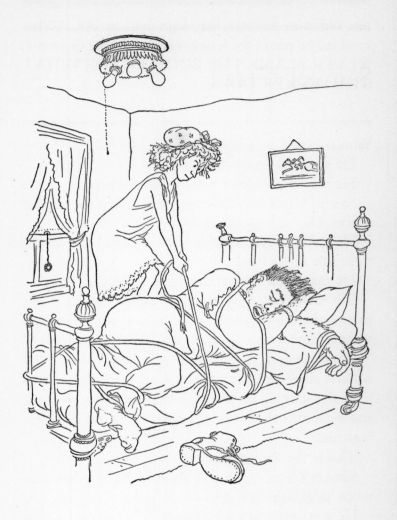

Samuel Graze

Samuel Graze was six-feet-three.

He weighed 250 pounds.

He was muscle-bound from the neck up.

Samuel Graze worked at the steel mill in the general offices. He made good money.

He had blue eyes, and blond hair, and a lump on the right side of his face.

He married a girl by the name of Magda Yust.

She was a nice girl, and had a good job in a department store when Samuel Graze married her. She weighed about ninety-two pounds with her hat on.

They were a strange-looking couple when they walked along the street, because of the difference in their size, but big men always like little bitsy women, and little men always go for women the size of a first baseman.

This is the way it is in life.

Samuel Graze got in the habit of beating his wife when he did not feel well.

He was nearly always ailing.

He would beat her with his fists, or with a broom-stick, or anything else that was handy around the house. He wore her down to sixty pounds, with her hat off.

Everybody in Our Town said it wasn't very nice of Samuel Graze to beat a woman no bigger than Magda. They said he ought to pick on a woman his size.

But everybody agreed that Samuel Graze was a pretty good matchmaker.

After they had been married fifteen years, Magda Graze got tired of being beat up. By this time there wasn't much of her left to beat.

One night, after a good beating, she said to Samuel Graze, Samuel, you have beaten me for the last time. If ever you raise a hand to me again I will kill you.

This made Samuel laugh heartily. He thought she was kidding.

The next night he came home a little tight after drinking whisky all day in a barroom, and he gave her a very fine beating and went to bed.

The Coroner looked at Samuel in the bed the next morning, and he said he had never in all his professional career seen a deceased as black and blue as Samuel. The Coroner said Samuel Graze looked as if somebody had been painting him.

But all that happened was that after Samuel Graze went to sleep, Magda tied him in the bed, so he could not wiggle loose, and then beat him to death with a big club.

Everybody in Our Town said it was a wonderful

feat for a woman no bigger than Magda Graze to swing a club that big long enough to kill a man the size of Samuel.

They let Magda Graze off with a reprimand, although some thought it was setting a bad example to the other women in Our Town whose husbands like to give them a beating now and then.

Pete Hankins

Poor Pete Hankins was a fine man. He drove the truck six years for Gene Carson the laundryman. Then Gene Carson died and the big Snow White laundry people got all Gene Carson's business. There was no job for Pete. It was a shame. He was a very fine man.

Pete went to New York. He got a job as a taxi driver. He was always a very good driver in Our Town. He never had an accident.

He is forty years of age and has four children in their teens. He has three girls and one boy.

He has a tough time getting along.

He wears a mustache and in the winter it collects icicles.

Pete owns his own taxicab but by the time he pays for his license, gas and repairs out of his earnings, he does not have much left for himself.

The cops are very mean to Pete. In New York City the cops are very mean to all taxicab drivers. The cops call all taxicab drivers by the same name. It is Hey You.

Some of the people who ride in Pete's taxicab are also very mean to him. They always think he is trying

13

to cheat them out of a larger fare on the meter when he happens to go a block out of the way.

The most Pete could cheat them out of even if he tried is about six cents and he never tries. He is a very honest taxicab driver. He has a little sign pasted up in front of him in his taxicab that reads honesty is the best policy.

Pete is always telling his son little Pete to live by this motto. Little Pete is sixteen. When his father tells him honesty is the best policy little Pete says, You have got something there, Pop.

One bitter cold morning around two o'clock when there was snow and ice in the streets, Pete delivered a fare to the Stork Club and then picked up a lady and gentleman in evening clothes who wanted to go to Jimmy Kelly's away down in Greenwich Village.

It was so cold Pete had more icicles on his mustache than usual.

The lady had on an ermine wrap and many jewels. The gentleman wore a high hat. They seemed in bad humor. When Pete's taxicab skidded a little on the ice the lady screamed and told him to be careful. The gentleman called him a bad name.

Pete said he was sorry but it was the fault of the ice. The lady wanted to know if he was trying to kill them. Pete thought of his children at home and said no, he did not want to kill anybody because he might get killed himself. The lady said she guessed he was just ignorant. The gentleman called him another bad name.

When Pete took a slightly longer route to avoid some bad streets going to Jimmy Kelly's the gentleman said he was trying to swindle him. Pete said all right if the gentleman thought that, he would knock off any difference the gentleman thought proper on the meter.

The lady told the gentleman not to argue with an ignorant taxi driver.

When they got to Jimmy Kelly's the gentleman paid just what was on the meter and would not give Pete a tip. The lady said, That is right, George, he does not deserve a tip, and Pete went back to his stand up our street wondering why the lady and gentleman should be so rude.

He happened to look in his cab and there on the seat was the lady's purse and when he opened to see if there was an address, he found it contained two thousand dollars in money and a big square diamond ring, but no address.

So Pete jumped on the seat of his cab and drove back to Jimmy Kelly's but the lady and gentleman had gone somewhere else and the head waiter thought it was El Morocco.

So Pete drove away uptown to El Morocco looking for the lady and gentleman. They were not there.

He drove all over town stopping in every night club. Finally he found them in the Club 18.

He called them out and returned the purse to the lady. She had not missed it as yet. She looked at Pete very suspiciously as she examined the contents and counted the money.

By this time Pete's mustache had so many icicles on it he could hardly open his mouth.

The gentleman looked at Pete very suspiciously too. Then they both went back into the Club 18 without even saying thank you to Pete. He thought they should have offered to pay him for the gas he used up looking for them.

The next day Pete was getting ready to go to work in his taxicab when his son little Pete came along and noticed the little sign pasted up in the cab and read it out loud and said, Pop, you have got something there, all right. Honesty is the best policy.

Pete just drove off to work.

Jeremiah Zore

Jeremiah Zore was a mean man. He was one of the six meanest men in Our Town.

He stood third on the list.

Jeremiah Zore had a thin body, thin hair, thin lips, and a thin soul.

He got rich through lending money on property, and squeezing every nickel he got hold of. He loved foreclosing mortgages and throwing people out of their homes on Christmas Eve.

He was mean to everybody, and especially to his wife, Mame Zore. She was married to Jeremiah for twenty-nine years, and never laughed once after the first two months of their marriage.

She had one new dress in six years, and she made it herself.

They had one child, a son named Jonathan, and Jeremiah Zore was kind to him on four different occasions in sixteen years. They were the only occasions that Jeremiah was kind to anybody or anything.

Jeremiah Zore was secretly proud of Jonathan, and tried to make friends with him, but he was so mean to Mame Zore that Jonathan hated him, and on his seventeenth birthday he ran away from home.

Some said Jeremiah Zore brooded over Jonathan running away and kept hoping he would return, but Jeremiah never let on to anybody. Meantime, he was getting meaner, and meaner, and richer and richer.

He knew that everybody in Our Town hated him, and one day he said he was going to build a monument to himself that would make Our Town remember him, anyway.

So he built a twenty-four story building on Commercial Avenue, with a tall tower on top of it.

It was the tallest building in our section of the state, and everybody in Our Town was quite proud of it until it was completed and Jeremiah Zore put his rents so low he almost ruined all the owners of the other downtown office buildings.

He admitted that this was his idea in the first place.

It was a beautiful building by day and would have been beautiful by night if Jeremiah had permitted the tower to be lighted up, but he was too stingy for that.

It shows you what a mean man he was.

Then one day Jeremiah lay dying, and he told Mame Zore his only wish was to see his son once more. He said he had never for a moment ceased thinking of Jonathan, who was a famous aviator, back East.

So Mame sent word to Jonathan and asked him to come as a favor to her and Jonathan sent word back he was flying his own plane to Our Town, and Jeremiah Zore cheered up and became so strong that there was great fear he would recover.

It was a black night, and storming heavily when Jonathan Zore arrived over Our Town in his plane, and flying very low looking for the landing field, he crashed into the tower on the Zore Building and was instantly killed.

He did not know the building had been erected and there was no light on the tower, so Jeremiah Zore died without seeing his son, Jonathan, after all.

Mrs. Judson

Mrs. Judson was a fine looking woman.

Her maiden name was Clucas.

Her father was a druggist.

She married a man named Sabin when she was about eighteen.

He traveled for a candy manufacturing concern.

She loved Simon Sabin very dearly. He was 5 feet 9½ inches tall, and weighed 160 pounds. He wore a black mustache.

They seemed to get along together all right. He was on the road a lot.

One day Simon Sabin went away on a trip, and did not came back. He did not even write his wife a letter. She liked to get letters, too.

There were various rumors about Simon Sabin. He was reported seen from time to time in this city and that. But the years went on and no definite word came from him, and many people decided that Simon Sabin must have met with foul play.

They sympathized deeply with his poor wife.

She bore up as well as could be expected.

After a lapse of twenty years, Mrs. Sabin became Mrs. Judson. She married Jeremiah Judson, the prin-

cipal of the East Side High School. He was a fine
man, quiet, and studious, and he often took Mrs.
Judson to the movies.

They were extremely happy. Mrs. Judson loved
the movies.

One day Simon Sabin came back to Our Town. He
had gray hair, and his mustache was now gray, and his
teeth were bad. He looked seedy.

He said he had been away on an unusually long
trip, but that he was glad to get back home. The
candy manufacturing company had failed during his
absence, and not many people remembered Simon
Sabin, but he did not mind.

He hurried to Mrs. Judson's house. She was greatly
surprised to see him, especially as she had been going
along thinking Simon Sabin was dead. She recalled
that she had not bothered to get a divorce from Simon
Sabin before marrying Jeremiah Judson.

This complicated the situation, and everybody
wondered what Mrs. Judson would do.

She listened a few minutes to Simon Sabin telling
her how glad he was to be home, then she picked up a
broom, and struck him over the head with it, and
continued striking him until Simon Sabin broke into
a run.

Mrs. Judson followed him as far as her gate, and
got in a few extra good belts at Simon Sabin with the

broom handle, and he kept running until he was out of the city limits. He has never since returned.

Most people said that Mrs. Judson did exactly right, although some of the ladies in Our Town said that she should have at least invited Simon Sabin in for a cup of tea, if only to find out where he had been all this time.

The Happiness Joneses

The Joneses were a happy family.

Everybody talked about how happy they were.

"As happy as the Joneses," was a saying in Our Town.

They were poor in this world's goods, but richer than the Rockefellers in happiness.

The Joneses were Stella, Bella, Ella, Nella, Fred, Ted, Ed, Jed, and Papa and Mamma Jones. The children were all pretty well grown, and most of them worked, and several lived together in a funny looking old frame house on Rambold street, and people used to pass that way just to see the Joneses in their happiness.

They were certainly a happy family.

In fact, they were known far and wide as the Happiness Joneses.

They loved one another dearly.

Some of the girls and boys were married and had children; others were of marriageable age, but these said they would never think of marrying, because they did not wish to leave the happy home on Rambold street.

One day a man by the name of Mr. Morgan, with

a taking smile, came along selling tickets on a big
sweepstake and all the Joneses chipped in a few cents
apiece and bought a ticket because they liked the way
Mr. Morgan talked.

Mr. Morgan was a slick fellow.

Some of the Joneses chipped in a few cents more
than the others to make up the full amount of the
ticket. It cost $2.60.

The ticket won $150,000.

That was a lot of money for Our Town.

It was a lot of money for any town.

Everybody said it meant the finish of the Happiness Joneses. Everybody said Stella, Bella, Ella, Nella,
Fred, Ted, Ed, Jed and Papa and Mamma Jones
would soon be quarreling like a lot of cats and dogs,
especially when those that contributed the most cents
got to figuring they were entitled to more of the swag.

But when the money came, the Joneses just put it
out on investment in a lump sum, and lived off the
income.

They did not quarrel at all, but continued as happy
as ever, even down to the grandchildren.

In fact, they were happier than ever, because they
now had enough money for all their needs, and did
not have to scrimp and save.

Everybody in Our Town was good and hot about
this.

Everybody said that nobody had a right to all that money, and happiness, too.

Some say now they do not believe the Joneses won any money, anyway, because they are so happy, even as long as this since they bought the ticket.

Everybody in Our Town really has been sore at the Joneses ever since.

Mrs. McGregor

Mrs. McGregor was quite a widow in Our Town.

She had a world of experience.

She was married to seven different men.

One died. Four ran away and got divorces from her, and she divorced the other two right in Our Town.

The names of Mrs. McGregor's husbands were Cadwallader, Kearns, Tilbury, Turnbull, Smith, Doyle and McGregor. Her maiden name was Suggs.

She was nothing extra for looks but men seemed to like to marry her.

Cadwallader was her first husband. He worked in a shoe store. He was one of the four that ran away. The others were Tilbury, Turnbull and Kearns. Doyle and McGregor were the ones she herself divorced.

She said they were guilty of mental cruelty.

She said Doyle smoked a pipe in bed and McGregor ate onions and limburger cheese and drank beer every night after getting through work.

He was a switchman in the Santa Fe yards.

Everybody agreed that Mrs. McGregor had grounds in this case.

She was a strapping big woman, with auburn hair and white teeth. She came of a good family in Our Town and was a fine housekeeper. She seemed to have plenty of good common sense.

Smith was her third husband.

Nobody in Our Town could remember much about him.

He was a salesman in an electrical fixtures store and was a little, quiet man who had nothing to say. He came from Salem, Massachusetts.

He was married to Mrs. McGregor about a year when he died of pneumonia and was buried in Riverview Cemetery. He came and went so rapidly that very few people in Our Town mentioned his name when calling the roll of Mrs. McGregor's husbands.

She rarely spoke of Smith.

She would talk about Cadwallader, Kearns, Tilbury, Turnbull, Doyle and McGregor and tell you what bums they were, yet never a word about Smith.

But every Sunday afternoon, rain or shine, Mrs. McGregor would go out to Riverview Cemetery and visit Smith's grave. Sometimes she would take flowers.

Joe Sneezbold, the superintendent of the cemetery, said she would sit beside the grave for hours at a time. She kept this up even when she was married to Tilbury, Kearns, Doyle and McGregor.

They did not mind much.

One day Joe Sneezebold remarked to Mrs. Mc-

Gregor that she must have loved Smith a great deal. She said no, she did not love him an extra lot. She said she did not love him any more than she loved any of her other husbands but she respected him more.

She said Smith was the only man she had ever known who occasionally asked her if she did not feel tired and that it rested her now to sit beside his grave.

Mrs. McGregor was regarded as a strange woman.

Doc Brackett

Doc Brackett didn't have black whiskers.

Nonetheless, he was a fine man.

He doctored in Our Town for many years. He doctored more people than any other doctor in Our Town but made less money.

That was because Doc Brackett was always doctoring poor people, who had no money to pay.

He would get up in the middle of the coldest night and ride twenty miles to doctor a sick woman, or child, or to patch up some fellow who got hurt.

Everybody in Our Town knew Doc Brackett's office over Rice's clothing store. It was up a narrow flight of stairs. His office was always filled with people. A sign at the foot of the stairs said: DR. BRACKETT, OFFICE UPSTAIRS.

Doc Brackett was a bachelor. He was once supposed to marry Miss Elvira Cromwell, the daughter of old Junius Cromwell, the banker, but on the day the wedding was supposed to take place Doc Brackett got a call to go out into the country and doctor a Mexican child.

Miss Elvira got sore at him and called off the wedding. She said that a man who would think more of a

Mexican child than of his wedding was no good. Many women in Our Town agreed with Miss Elvira Cromwell, but the parents of the Mexican child were very grateful to Doc Brackett when the child recovered.

For forty years, the lame, and the halt, and the blind of Our Town had climbed up and down the stairs to Doc Brackett's office.

He never turned away anybody.

Some said Doc Brackett was a loose character, because he liked to drink whisky and play poker in the back rooms of saloons.

But he lived to be seventy years old, and then one day he keeled over on the sofa in his office and died. By this time his black hair had turned white.

Doc Brackett had one of the biggest funerals ever seen in Our Town. Everybody went to pay their last respects when he was laid out in Gruber's undertaking parlors. He was buried in Riverview Cemetery.

There was talk of raising money to put a nice tombstone on Doc Brackett's grave as a memorial. The talk got as far as arguing about what should be carved on the stone about him. Some thought poetry would be very nice.

Doc Brackett hated poetry.

The matter dragged along and nothing whatever was done.

Then one day George Gruber, the undertaker, said

that Doc Brackett's memorial was already over his grave, with an epitaph and all. George Gruber said the Mexican parents of the child Doc Brackett saved years ago had worried about him having no tombstone.

They had no money themselves, so they took the sign from the foot of the stairs at Doc Brackett's office and stuck it over his grave. It read: DR. BRACKETT, OFFICE UPSTAIRS.

Officer Lipscomber

Freddie Lipscomber used to be a policeman in Our Town. His older brother Howie Lipscomber still lives here over Earnshaw's Drug Store.

Howie is not what you would call good-looking but he is a fine citizen. Freddie was a very handsome man and had a different personality. Howie is very quiet.

Freddie quit being a policeman in Our Town very suddenly. That was seven years ago. Some people say he had to quit because he was paying more attention to Widow Farnsworth than to his job. Widow Farnsworth is a very beautiful woman.

Howie is very devoted to his brother and he always says to this day that the widow was only a good friend. He says Freddie's only trouble is that he has a heart of gold.

Freddie is now a policeman in New York. He visits Howie every summer at the end of July. Policemen in New York are very busy on holidays. More than a million tourists visit New York every day, especially July 4th.

Freddie has a fine job. The New York police are

the highest paid in the world. Freddie is called Officer Lipscomber now.

He has a four-room apartment, a blond wife and an angora cat. The cat's name is Bella. It likes liver.

Officer Lipscomber is thirty years old and has been in the police department five years. He is a hard-working, conscientious policeman and loves his wife and Mayor LaGuardia. She allows him three dollars per week for spending money. He does not care for Bella, and that is strictly between Officer Lipscomber and his wife.

He endeavors to bring the human equation into the discharge of his police duties. He always tries to put himself in the other fellow's place in a situation involving a breach of the law and possible arrest.

That is what Officer Lipscomber says. I try to put myself in the other fellow's place.

He is a fine figure of a man in his uniform. Ladies often turn around and look at him the second time but Officer Lipscomber does not look at them more than once. He is ambitious to command the department some day.

He does not make many arrests. He says by putting himself in the other fellow's place he usually finds an arrest unnecessary. He gets more sleep than most policemen who have to get up early and go to court to testify in arrests. That is why Officer Lipscomber always looks healthy.

His wife is very proud of him. Her name is Sheila. When he commands the Police Department, he is going to move out of our street to a suburb where Bella will have a yard to play in.

One night Officer Lipscomber was patrolling his beat on Ninth Avenue, trying doors as he went along to see if any had accidently been left unlocked.

It was a cold night and he was wishing Sheila would allow him a dollar more per week for spending money. It was something to think about to pass the time away. A policeman must think of something to pass the time away. He thought how well he could use a dollar more per week.

He found the door of a small butcher shop unlocked and looking through the window, Officer Lipscomber saw an elderly little man with a white mustache and spectacles going through the cash register.

Officer Lipscomber entered the shop with drawn revolver and told the little man to put up his hands. He told the little man to consider himself under arrest. He said, You ought to be ashamed to be a burglar at your time of life.

The little man was badly frightened. Then he said he and his wife Esther owned the butcher shop and that business was good but that Esther allowed him only two dollars per week for spending money. He said he really needed more than that so he was taking some odd change out of the cash register.

Officer Lipscomber sat down and thought this over. He put himself in the other fellow's place. He could see that a businessman like a butcher would need more than two dollars per week spending money when a policeman like himself could conveniently use more than three. He thought of his wife, Sheila.

He told the little man that the thing for them to do was to go to the little man's house and wake up his wife Esther and have her identify him and everything would be all right. The little man said yes, but then they would have to tell her he had been found in the shop and she would suspect right away he had been in there to rob the register and he would be worse off than ever.

Officer Lipscomber thought this over, too. He put himself in the other fellow's place again. He thought of his wife Sheila. He told the little man he could see where he was between the devil and the deep blue sea and for him to go on about his business and forget the interruption.

Officer Lipscomber returned to trying doors. He congratulated himself on saving a fellow human being great embarrassment by putting himself in the other fellow's place. He thought of his wife Sheila.

The next day Officer Lipscomber was spoken to quite severely by his superior because of the burglary of a butcher shop on his beat with the loss of $108 cash money. The owner of the butcher shop was around to the police station making a big complaint.

The owner's name was Goochman. He was a big fat man without a mustache. Officer Lipscomber asked him if he had a wife named Esther and Goochman said no he never had a wife and what business was it of Officer Lipscomber's anyway? He wanted to know where Officer Lipscomber was when the burglary came off. He said he was going to see Mayor LaGuardia.

Officer Lipscomber has made more arrests since then than any man in the department. He waits until he gets them in jail before he puts himself in the other fellow's place.

He asked his wife Sheila for an extra dollar on his allowance but she said no.

Marigold and Maidie So

Marigold and Maidie So left Our Town three years ago. That is their name. An S, an O—SO. You pronounce it So.

Maidie did not want to go to New York, but Marigold said Our Town was too confining.

Many people did not like Marigold because she took that attitude. They liked Maidie much better. But Maidie was a devoted sister and went to New York with Marigold.

Marigold is twenty-two years old and very beautiful. She knows it. She is employed in a large department store. She is in beauty preparations. Cosmetics. Perfumes. Things like that. She works there all day long. Once in a while she finds time to wait on the customers.

Marigold So loves the movies. She used to go every night with some one of the boys up our street. They are nice boys. They were proud to take a girl as beautiful as Marigold So to the movies. Then it got around that she would not play hands. She only wanted to look at the pictures.

This hurt her standing up our street.

Willie Feener heard the reports and said, Oh that's

what you guys say. Wait until you hear from the old master.

Willie Feener meant himself.

He took Marigold to the movies and then to a chop suey joint and spent three six-bits on her and reported her a real pain in the Adam's Apple. We do not know what Marigold So reported about Willie, but her brother, Zack, looked Willie up the next day. You should have seen Willie's eye.

Marigold's sister Maidie is all right. She is a year younger than Marigold and not so beautiful but all right. She said the trouble with Marigold was that she was too romantic. Maidie said Marigold was waiting for a dream prince to come along and claim her and that she hoped he would look like Franchot Tone.

Maidie said Franchot Tone was Marigold's idea of a dream prince, but that she would probably settle for Douglas Fairbanks, Jr., or Tyrone Power. Maidie said Marigold read all the movie fan magazines and knew plenty about the actors and actresses of the screen but what did that get her?

Maidie said, Give me one of the boys from up our street any time, even Willie Feener. Maidie is all right. She is 100 per cent.

One afternoon Marigold So was working in the department store when a quiet young man came to her beauty preparations counter. Cosmetics. Per-

fumes. Things like that. He said he wanted to buy
some perfume for an old lady.

Marigold's mind was miles away. She was dreaming
of her dream prince. She was dreaming of Franchot
Tone. She heard the quiet young man's request as in
a dream and set out a bottle of high-powered scent
for him to sniff at.

The quiet young man said that might be all right
for the flashier Harlem trade but would hardly do
for an old lady. Marigold came out of her dream
and got right snippy with the young man. She
thought it was most inconsiderate of him interrupt-
ing her dream of Franchot Tone.

She put him in his place in no time. She made
that quiet young man slink away. He did not buy
any perfume. Marigold was about to return to
dreaming of Franchot Tone when she noticed that a
floorwalker was talking to the young man and show-
ing so much politeness to him that she knew the
young man must be some pumpkins.

She waited until the young man had departed and
then she called the floorwalker over and asked him
who he was. The floorwalker said, Why, that was
Mr. Franchot Tone, the actor.

Marigold then remembered that she had sensed
something vaguely familiar about the quiet young
man when she was putting him in his place. She

fainted dead away. The floorwalker's name was Honeycott.

When Marigold got home that evening, her sister Maidie was just leaving the house. She said she was going to a movie with Willie Feener. Marigold said Willie Feener was a roughneck and that Maidie ought to have more self respect than to go anywhere with him. Marigold said remember how Brother Zack had to give Willie an eye.

Maidie said well he may be a roughneck but he has just learned that his Uncle Fred up in Maine died leaving him a million and a half. Maidie said, Willie and I are going to be married, but Brother Zack will never be permitted to visit us.

Marigold fainted dead away again. Her mother said it was probably the heat. Her father said no, she must have eaten something that did not agree with her. Her brother Zack said, I don't care what it was. She has put me in Dutch with Willie Feener the rest of my life.

Maidie played hands so hard with Willie Feener in the movies that she broke the third finger of his right hand for him. Maidie is all right. She is 100 per cent.

Sterling Curlew

Sterling Curlew was a traveling man.

He was a nice fellow.

He was on the road for a baking company.

He sold crackers, and similar products.

Sterling Curlew had a wife, whose name was Aileen. She had red hair, and was young, and very lively.

They lived in a little house at the far end of Commercial Street.

When Sterling Curlew returned home from a trip, he would knock at the front door of his house.

Then he would run around to the back door of the house with a big club, and nail anybody that came out that way.

Sometimes Sterling Curlew had no luck. That would be when Aileen didn't happen to be home.

Sterling Curlew loved Aileen dearly.

One night he nailed Ardmore Klung with his big club and broke Ardmore Klung's collarbone for him. This caused gossip in Our Town, because Ardmore Klung was president of the Klung Laundry Company, and very prominent.

Some said Sterling Curlew had gone too far with his club.

They said he ought to first see who he was hitting.

Others said Sterling Curlew was quite within his rights. They said he was entitled to hit anything that came out of his back door.

Ardmore Klung went to St. Mary's Hospital, and Sterling Curlew filed suit against him in the district court for $20,000 damages for the alienation of Aileen's affections.

Aileen went home to her mother, Mrs. Wilbur H. Stogan, who was no bargain, either.

Everybody in Our Town took sides about the suit, especially the women. They said Sterling Curlew was entitled to justice because of this snake, Ardmore Klung, sneaking into his little home during his absence, and stealing his wife's affections.

But before the case came to trial, Sterling Curlew's wife, Aileen, skipped out with a dentist by the name of Dr. Ichabod Joller, who was boarding at her mother's, and nobody ever heard from her again.

Sterling Curlew was naturally greatly depressed, as his suit had to be dismissed, and he had to pay the costs.

Then Ardmore Klung got out of the hospital and sued Sterling Curlew for $5,000 damages for breaking his collarbone, and the jury returned a verdict in favor of Ardmore Klung for the whole amount.

Sterling Curlew was five years in paying off the judgment, and he became quite a woman hater.

Doc Mindler

Doc Mindler was our County Physician.

He was a nice man.

He came to Our Town from the East for his health. Four years after he arrived he was elected County Physician on the Democratic ticket.

It was a year when the Democrats didn't figure they had any more chance than a snowball in Hades, and they were nominating anybody who would take a nomination.

All the other Democratic physicians in Our Town were pretty hot when it came out that Doc Mindler was elected, but they were not any hotter than the Democratic business men who refused to run for Sheriff, and Assessor, and the other offices.

Doc Mindler was a young fellow, and right good looking, and he was single. He had a Harvard accent. He got it going to Harvard College.

A lot of women in Our Town made sheep's eyes at Doc Mindler, but he would have no part of them. This was considered strange, as some of the women of Our Town are not hard to take.

Then it leaked out that Doc Mindler was fond of a woman by the name of Mrs. Gershing, who was

the wife of Joe Gershing, the dentist. They were
separated, but not divorced, because Joe said he had
scruples about divorce. It was the only thing Joe
was ever known to have any scruples about.

Doc Mindler was seen coming out of Mrs. Gershing's house late one night, and it created great
scandal in Our Town. The women who had been
making sheep's eyes at Doc Mindler said they were
probably living in sin. The other Democratic physicians said it was an awful disgrace to have such a man
representing the profession in office.

Doc Mindler was pretty sore about all this talk,
especially when it was taken up by a lot of prominent
business men, who talked of taking steps to get him
removed from office. He said he didn't mind about
himself, but was thinking of Mrs. Gershing. Doc
Mindler said she was as pure as the driven snow, and
perhaps purer. Doc Mindler said he would get even
with the whole town for this.

At two o'clock one Sunday morning, Doc Mindler
slapped a quarantine on the entire district of Our
Town that was known as The Line. It was where
the hot spots and gambling halls were located. Doc
Mindler said he had discovered a Mexican woman
there suffering from smallpox.

The quarantine was enforced by deputy sheriffs
armed with shotguns. It created considerable excitement, because over one hundred prominent citizens

of Our Town were caught in the quarantine, including many of those who had been talking about Doc Mindler and Mrs. Gershing. By daylight there was so much scandal in so many of our best families that Doc Mindler and Mrs. Gershing were entirely forgotten, and were not remembered until two years later when they got married.

Doc Mindler kept the quarantine on until noon the next day when he said he had learned that the Mexican woman had chicken pox and not smallpox, although the head nurse at St. Joseph's Hospital afterwards said Doc Mindler must have known about it five days before when the Mexican woman was first brought to his attention in the hospital.

Mrs. Pilplay

Mrs. Pilplay wasn't so young, but she still looked good. She liked dancing.

After Mr. Pilplay died she said good-by to Our Town and went to New York. She said that a lonely widow could get along better in New York. Mr. Pilplay was a farsighted man and had a large insurance policy.

Mrs. Pilplay is going on forty years of age and keeps her hair the same color the year around.

She has a nice shape when she gets it all buckled in and a cheerful smile. She has a four-room apartment, a maid and an old Pomeranian dog. The dog's name is Fluff. Everybody wishes to destroy Fluff on sight.

Mrs. Pilplay learned the rumba from a teacher at ten dollars per hour. She had all the motions down fine. There are a lot of motions to the rumba. First you go thisaway. Then you go thataway. Mrs. Pilplay used to go every night to a place where they had a rumba band and put it on good. She got a little hard of hearing from listening to rumba bands.

She knew a lot of jolly fellows who were always willing to go and do the rumba with her. She paid the tabs. That was only fair, because she is a widow and her competition was keen. She started running out of money not long ago and decided that it might be a smart idea to marry a provider.

She met a millionaire named Julius in the Stork Club one night and he fell in love with her. She looked good. Julius was sixty-six years old and an awful chromo but he was a millionaire. Mrs. Pilplay knew there was no sense in a widow being choosy about a millionaire's looks.

Everybody up our street was rooting for Mrs. Pilplay. We thought if she got Julius she might move to a more aristocratic neighborhood and take Fluff with her.

Old Julius's relatives were pretty sore. They had been waiting around with their tongues hanging out for years for him to die and leave them his dough. They hated to see Mrs. Pilplay cutting in on them. A granddaughter named Mrs. Vazzo was real nasty to Mrs. Pilplay one night in El Morocco. Mrs. V. called Mrs. P. a gold digger. Mrs. P. laughed and said bah.

Julius was a sedate old fellow. He did not dance the rumba. He did not dance anything. He just sat around. He said he was too old to dance. Mrs. Pilplay said nonsense, he was just the right age for dancing. She made him go to her teacher and take rumba lessons. The way Julius danced the rumba should be declared unconstitutional. He kept falling apart. The teacher raised his fee to $20 per hour but gave Mrs. Pilplay a finnif as commission.

She made Julius keep practicing the rumba until he got pretty good for a man sixty-six years old. That is not too good. He commenced looking younger. He began acting younger. He said he felt younger. That is what the rumba will do for a man. He said he would always be grateful to Mrs. Pilplay for taking him in hand and teaching him how to get some enjoyment out of life when everybody else thought he was a goner.

Mrs. Vazzo came around to see Mrs. Pilplay and apologized for her cracks in El Morocco. She said she was grateful to Mrs. Pilplay for rejuvenating Grandfather and that all the rest of his family were grateful, too.

She was right nice to Mrs. Pilplay. Afterwards Mrs. Pilplay found out that Julius's family physician, Dr. Furor, had told the family that all they had to do was to hope Mrs. Pilplay kept that old fugitive from a graveyard doing the rumba long enough and his heart would give out sure pop.

Julius got to liking the rumba so well that he not only wanted to dance it all night but all day too. That is what the rumba will do for a man. Mrs. Pilplay commenced to look a little run-down. She got bags under her eyes. Her feet took to hurting her. She had to pull up on Julius occasionally and spend all her time in bed.

Up our street we kept rooting for Mrs. Pilplay but we could see that she was losing her old zip. We were sorry but not surprised when we heard in the papers that Julius had eloped with a young cigarette girl named Maria who could rumba all hours. She ought to. She is a Cuban. It was a big story in the papers. They did not mention one break Mrs. Pilplay got when she was going around with Julius. She did not have to pay those tabs.

Mrs. Pilplay still lives up our street. She goes with Julius's family physician, Dr. Furor, now and may marry him. He is no great catch. A lot of his patients owe him money that he will never get. Mrs. Pilplay and Dr. Furor go out dancing once in a while but they never rumba. They stick to waltzes. She looks good again.

Mrs. Pilplay still has Fluff. She found Sully, the cop on the beat up our street, trying to teach Fluff to sit up the other night. She asked Sully to quit that. She said Fluff is an old dog and that it is silly to teach an old dog new tricks.

That is what the rumba will do for a man.

Sheriff Harding

John Harding was a very serious young man.

He had no sense of humor whatever.

John Harding believed that all laws were made to be enforced.

He was always mentioning this idea.

John Harding took an interest in politics, and attended conventions, and made speeches. He was always making speeches about law enforcement. John Harding was a Republican.

Finally, one day, Vic Morton suggested that John Harding would make a good sheriff. Vic Morton was a Republican leader. He ran a filling station. He was a great joker, and was half joking when he suggested John Harding for sheriff.

John Harding did not want to be sheriff. He was doing all right as assistant manager of Shuman's wholesale grocery. He had a chance to be manager some day. He was very popular with his employers and associates.

John Harding was very popular with everybody.

Our Town needed a good sheriff, as the newspapers were making a fuss about Sheriff Sid Carroll not enforcing the law. The newspapers in Our Town made a fuss about enforcing the law at least once a year on general principles.

The Republicans nominated John Harding for sheriff, and he finally accepted, but he said if he was elected he would enforce the law. Vic Morton made the nominating speech for John Harding, and laughed heartily when he heard what John Harding said.

Three days after John Harding took office, Ad Attle, a colored fellow, shot and killed George Dibblee, because George struck him over the head with a jack handle.

George had a hot temper.

He did not know Ad had a gun.

Ad was arrested by Deputy Sheriff Karns, and taken to the county jail and locked up. There was much indignation over the killing, as George Dibblee was very popular in Our Town, and it was decided to get up a mob and lynch Ad Attle. There had not been any excitement in Our Town for weeks.

Vic Morton got up the mob.

It marched up to the county jail and sent in word to hand over Ad Attle. John Harding came out on the steps and said the request would not be granted. John Harding said he was the sheriff and sworn to do his duty, and that he would kill the first man who tried to break into the jail.

Vic Morton laughed.

Vic Morton said, Come on, boys, and started up the steps of the county jail.

John Harding shot him through the head with a .38-calibre Smith & Wesson.

This broke up the mob.

John Harding was impeached later on and fired out of his job as sheriff for killing Vic Morton. He has been a bum around Our Town ever since.

Everybody said John Harding had his gall shooting the man who first suggested that he be made sheriff.

Boswell Van Dusen

Boswell Van Dusen was the owner and editor of the *Morning Chief*.

He was a very nice fellow.

He always spoke well of everybody.

His wife's name was Myrtle. That is all we have to say about Mrs. Van Dusen.

Boswell Van Dusen's motto for the *Morning Chief* was, If you can't boost, don't knock.

He was a great believer in sweetness and light. He had shaved off his mustache and he didn't have much hair on his head. He claimed there was some good in everybody. He always wrote nice things about everybody in the *Morning Chief*. He never had a bad word for anyone.

Boswell Van Dusen had a tough time making ends meet with the *Morning Chief*.

The business men in our town advertised in it when they felt like it. Generally, they didn't feel like it. They knew Boswell Van Dusen wouldn't bother them in the *Morning Chief*.

Nobody paid much attention to him or his paper, because everybody understood that Boswell Van Dusen was a kind man and very harmless, and would give anybody who got married a nice notice, and anybody who died a lovely obituary, and would keep anything out of the paper that anybody wanted kept out.

Then one day Boswell Van Dusen got to thinking things over. He realized that the *Morning Chief* was dying the death of a rag baby, and that he himself was in danger of starving.

He said to himself, To hell with sweetness and light, it ain't no good. He began knocking the brains out of everybody.

He called the politicians liars, and thieves, and cutthroats.

He said half the people in Our Town ought to be in jail.

Everybody felt that this statement was a slight exaggeration on Boswell Van Dusen's part.

Everybody said the number was only one-third, at most.

There was some talk of killing Boswell Van Dusen. He said he didn't care, he would just as soon be killed as starve to death.

He wouldn't keep anything out of the paper any more. He began printing news about the leading men in Our Town.

This was very embarrassing to them. They began putting ads in the *Morning Chief*.

The politicians commenced thinking of Boswell Van Dusen when they were cutting anything up.

In six months the *Morning Chief* was the most prosperous paper in the State.

Boswell Van Dusen put in a new press, and bought Walter Winchell's column.

Everybody in Our Town is very proud of the *Morning Chief*.

Everybody says Boswell Van Dusen is a great editor, even if he doesn't ever have a kind word for anyone.

Dr. Davenport

Dr. Davenport was a wonderful man.

He came to Our Town fresh from medical college, and opened an office.

He soon had a great practice.

Dr. Davenport had some money of his own, and he never sent a bill for his service to anybody that he knew was a little pressed, trusting them to pay him when things got better for them.

So, of course, nobody ever paid Dr. Davenport.

Often he took care of hospital bills out of his own pocket.

Everybody said Dr. Davenport was a great philanthropist and a fine man.

The only patients that ever got statements from Dr. Davenport were those he knew could afford to pay, but very few of them ever remembered to settle with him, because they knew he had a little money and would never press them.

Dr. Davenport was a gentle, kindly soul. He always spoke well of everybody.

His charity saved many lives in Our Town.

When the depression came on, it wiped out all of Dr. Davenport's resources and left him without a dime. He was greatly surprised at this, as he had always been accustomed to having a little money whenever he needed it.

He decided to collect some of what was coming to him, and looking over his books he discovered that he had $123,876.70 outstanding after fifteen years of practice in Our Town, much of it due from well-known citizens.

So Dr. Davenport sent out a few bills, though he hated to do it. In fact, he felt embarrassed about it. Those who received the bills were not embarrassed. They were only surprised. They threw the bills in the wastebasket and forgot all about them at once.

Things got pretty bad for Dr. Davenport. In fact, he was almost starving. He went around looking seedy, and forlorn, and most people said it served him right for being such a bad businessman and not attending to his affairs better.

Then one morning, Dr. Davenport got up very early, and borrowed a six-shooter from a friend on the police force, and went around to the citizens who owed him money, and told each and every one that he would blow their heads off if they did not pay him at once.

Dr. Davenport had $6,876.70 in his pocket by nightfall and was able to eat his first square meal in nine months, but he never had much standing in Our

Town afterward, as the better class would not patronize him.

They said a doctor who expected to get paid for his services must be crazy. The seventy cents Dr. Davenport collected from Mrs. Gabe Wheeler, whose husband, Gabe Wheeler, had borrowed the money from Dr. Davenport seven years before to buy rough-on-rats, which Gabe took himself.

Mrs. Wheeler always felt grateful to Dr. Davenport for that, even though she had neglected to pay back the money.

Mrs. Bogane

Jack Bogane died at the age of sixty-six.

He was a big ranchman.

He owned the 7—2 Ranch, twenty-six miles south-west of Our Town.

Jack Bogane left a wife when he died. Her name was Hester, and she had been married to Jack Bogane for thirty-two years.

He met her in Denver when she was eighteen years old. Hester was then working as a chambermaid in a hotel. She had been working as a chambermaid or a waitress since she was fourteen.

She was an orphan.

Jack Bogane was already a fairly successful ranchman when he married Hester.

He took her at once to the 7—2 Ranch, and for the next thirty-two years Hester did all the cooking for a ranch crew of anywhere from ten to twenty men, and most of the other housework.

Jack Bogane was a nice fellow, but he was a little near, and he didn't see any reason why he should employ a cook and other help when he had a wife.

So from four o'clock in the morning until nine o'clock at night, Hester Bogane was cooking, and washing dishes, and making beds, and waiting on men.

She never had time to have any children.

She never saw a movie until she was past forty.

She was sixty years old when Jack died and looked eighty.

He left her the 7—2 Ranch, and a lot of money.

She sold the ranch at once, and moved into Our Town, and bought a big house, and employed ten servants, all women, although there was no one else living in the house but her.

She seldom left the house, and people in Our Town considered her eccentric.

There was a rumor that she had all her meals in bed, and that she would not lift a hand to do anything for herself, but always had a couple of her servants around her to do it for her.

It was said that Mrs. Bogane would not even pick up a handkerchief she had dropped, but would ring for a servant. She had so many servants that they got in one another's way.

One day some distant relatives of Mrs. Bogane appeared in Our Town, and hired John Getty, the lawyer, to bring suit in court to have a conservator appointed for her on the ground that she was out of her mind.

They said the number of servants she employed proved it.

But when the case came to trial before Judge Organ in the county court, he threw it out when Mrs. Bogane went on the stand and said she felt that after waiting on other people most of her life, she had a right to be waited on herself the few years that she had left to her.

When they heard Mrs. Bogane's viewpoint, everybody in Our Town, especially the women, said Judge Organ did the proper thing, and he was invited to address several women's clubs on the subject of equality of the sexes.

Moreover, everybody in Our Town said it served the relatives just right when it came out after Mrs. Bogane's death that she had left her fortune to found a home for worn-out servant girls.

Sam Crable

Sam Crable killed Beaver McClintock.

Sam used a .44-calibre Colt revolver.

He told Beaver McClintock three different times to quit fooling around Mrs. Crable.

Beaver owned the McClintock Hotel. He was standing in front of the hotel at 7 P. M. picking his teeth, after having enjoyed a nice dinner.

Sam Crable came along on the other side of the street, and hollered, Oh, Beaver, and when Beaver looked up, Sam shot him between the eyes.

It was just coming on dusk, and everybody thought that was pretty good shooting, considering.

Beaver fell down and died right in front of his hotel. The incident gave the hotel a bad name for years. Sam kept on walking until he met a policeman, and said, I just killed Beaver McClintock, and the policeman said, That is against the law, and I will have to lock you up.

He liked Sam Crable.

Nonetheless, he locked him up in the city jail, and Mrs. Crable went to see Sam right away and bawled him out for shooting Beaver McClintock. She said Beaver was nothing to her but a friend.

The shooting of Beaver McClintock caused talk. Some said Sam Crable ought to be lynched.

Book Anderson, who ran the Globe cigar store, and was very religious, said no, it was better to let Sam live, because his conscience would be his own punishment.

Book Anderson said that everybody knows that a man who kills another man never afterwards closes his eyes, even in sleep. Book said that a man who kills another is haunted by his conscience all the rest of his days, so his eyes are always open and staring.

This led to quite an argument.

Some agreed with Book, but others said it would be impossible for a man to go on for years with his eyes open, so finally somebody suggested that a good way to settle the argument would be to go around to the city jail and find out if Sam Crable's eyes were open or closed while he was sleeping.

Quite a party went.

Book Anderson led the way, telling about cases he knew of men who had done a little killing never again closing their eyes.

Just outside the city jail they ran into Officer Carter and Sam Crable, just getting into an automobile. Officer Carter had the come-alongs on Sam Crable, and Sam looked somewhat embarrassed at seeing his old friends.

Officer Carter explained that he was transferring

Sam Crable from the city jail to the county jail. He said Sam slept so sound and snored so loud in the city jail that the other prisoners complained.

Book Anderson did not bother to ask Officer Carter if Sam slept with his eyes open or closed.

Ancil Toombs

Ancil Toombs was N. G.

In spades.

Ancil Toombs never worked a day in his life.

He was forty-five years old.

Ancil Toombs was tall, and thin, and had long black hair. His wife, Amy Toombs, cut it for him once a month.

Amy Toombs had a little millinery store on Commercial street, and worked hard all day long, while Ancil Toombs hung out around the Grand Billiard Academy playing pool. He spent the greater part of his days and evenings at the billiard academy.

Ancil Toombs was a first-class pool player. He could run off fifteen from the break.

Ancil Toombs' wife, Amy, had to hurry home from her little store every evening to get Ancil's supper. Ancil never went near the store except to get a half dollar off Amy.

Some people in Our Town said Ancil Toombs ought to be shot, but others claimed he wasn't worth shooting.

Everybody agreed that he was N. G.

In spades.

One day the Democrats were looking around for a candidate for Congressman.

The Democrats in Our Town had no chance to win the election, so they nominated candidates for the different offices who had plenty of time on their hands.

Somebody suggested Ancil Toombs, and Ancil Toombs was nominated by acclamation.

He was inclined to be sore about it at first, as he said it was a reflection on his industry. Everybody in Our Town knew the Democrats were only nominating candidates who had nothing else to do but be candidates.

It happened to be the year Roosevelt swept the country, and Ancil Toombs was elected. His wife was greatly relieved because it meant Ancil would be in Washington most of the time and could not bother her for half dollars.

Everybody said Ancil Toombs would be a joke as a Congressman, but they were mistaken. He became the greatest authority in Congress on the drafting of income tax bills.

Everybody in Our Town is now very proud of Ancil Toombs and his record in Washington. He will be endorsed by both the Democrats and the Republicans at the next election.

Amy Vederman

Amy Vederman was a homely girl. She was the home-liest girl in Our Town. In fact, she was the homeliest girl in our county.

Some said she was the homeliest girl in our state.

Jack Moroso, the gambler, offered to take a price that she was the homeliest girl west of the Mississippi, bar Iowa.

Jack Moroso came from Iowa.

But in spite of being homely, Amy Vederman had the happiest disposition of any girl in Our Town.

She was happy about everything.

She knew she was homely, but she did not worry about it. She was happy she had her health. She was happy she had enough to eat. She was happy she was alive.

Amy Vederman's father was Vincent J. Vederman, who had a nice wholesale furniture business. He was able to give Amy everything she wanted. She moved in good circles. She went to all the dances at the Country Club, although nobody ever danced with her because she was so homely.

She was a wallflower from infancy.

She was born to be an old maid.

But she was happy just the same.

She was so happy that everybody said it was a sin and a shame she was not better looking. Many of the prettiest girls in Our Town had terrible dispositions, but they always got attention.

When Amy Vederman was about twenty-five years old, there was a big dance at the Country Club, and Billy Chairs got the idea of making Amy Vederman the belle of the evening without her knowing it.

Billy Chairs was a handsome young fellow who worked in the Stockgrowers' National Bank. He was very popular with all the girls and had a kind heart. He said that a girl as happy as Amy Vederman deserved more enjoyment in life, so he took all the girls and boys in the Country Club bunch to help out in his idea.

The girls did not mind Amy Vederman, she was so homely.

So the night of the dance, Amy Vederman found herself constantly the center of an admiring group of young fellows, while the other girls sat on the sidelines.

She had a partner for every dance. The boys waited on her, hand and foot, and took her out under the trees for strolls between dances, and in general made her feel like she was the queen of the occasion.

They thought they were doing a good deed and adding to Amy Vederman's happiness, but before the dance was over, she was barely nodding to the other girls.

She thought it was all on the level, and she got so swelled up that nobody could get near enough to hand her a ripe apple. She never learned it was all a put-up job.

Amy Vederman is now forty-three years old, and is the unhappiest woman in the whole United States.

She never knew another happy moment from the night of the dance because she has never been able to enjoy another triumph like that.

Everybody in Our Town always said that Billy Chairs was a mean fellow for doing such a thing to Amy Vederman.

Peter Chowles

Peter Chowles was a nice man. He was also a first-class barber.

He had No. 1 chair in the Star Barber Shop. Everybody liked Peter Chowles.

He was always singing as he worked. He had a low, bass voice. But he gave good shaves and haircuts.

Peter Chowles was married to Letitia Soors, who was very beautiful. Her father was old Sim Soors, the plumber. Sim was no account, but Letitia was an excellent cook, and would have made Peter Chowles a splendid wife if she hadn't been so beautiful.

Everybody but Peter Chowles knew about Letitia and Irving Burkestrom, who was president of the Burkestrom Dry Goods Company. He had plenty of money, and a black mustache.

Irving Burkestrom was very proud of his black mustache. He would go to the Star Barber Shop every day, and have Peter Chowles shave him, and wax his black mustache, and then Irving Burkestrom would go out in his big car and meet Letitia Chowles, and they would have a good time together.

Irving Burkestrom said Peter Chowles was the best barber in the world. He liked to have Peter

Chowles sing to him while he was getting shaved and having his black mustache waxed.

Irving Burkestrom was about forty years old, and seemed very healthy. He always boasted he never had been sick a day in his life. Once he chinned himself nine times hand-running on a door to prove how well he was.

Everybody in Our Town was therefore greatly surprised when Irving Burkestrom died in Peter Chowles' barber chair one day when Peter Chowles was shaving him and singing to him.

Peter Chowles hadn't got around to waxing Irving Burkestrom's black mustache when he noticed Irving Burkestrom was dead in the chair. It was a shock to Peter Chowles. He hated to lose such a good customer as Irving Burkestrom.

The Coroner held an inquest over Irving Burkestrom, and it was decided that he had died of heart disease. He was buried in Riverview Cemetery and Peter Chowles sent a nice wreath.

Letitia Chowles did not even attend the funeral.

Someone once asked Peter Chowles what he was singing to Irving Burkestrom when he died. Peter never told anybody but Letitia that he was singing to a tune he made up himself for the exact words of a love letter from Irving Burkestrom to her that Peter found in her handbag, and that all the time he was singing he was keeping time by stropping his razor.

Judge Juggins

Judge Juggins was a just man.

He presided over the District Court in Our Town for years.

Everybody voted for Judge Juggins when he came up for re-election, because they knew him as a just man.

Besides, he looked fine sitting up there on the Judge's bench in the District Court. Everybody felt proud of Judge Juggins, and used to take visitors to his court room to hear him sentence somebody to prison because he always did it in such a splendid manner, and was so just.

He gave old Fred Peppering ten years in prison for stabbing his brother to death with an ice pick, when he might have made it life, but Fred was ninety-four years old at the time and a little crazy, and Judge Juggins said he felt Fred would not live out the sentence as it was.

That is how just Judge Juggins was.

He could have given Mrs. Waggoner ten years the time she married Bill Waggoner, thinking her first husband, Joe Hemps, was killed in the war, because bigamy is a very serious offense, but Judge Juggins

only made it eight years, as Mrs. Waggoner had five
small children, and he did not wish to be severe on a
mother.

That is how just Judge Juggins was.

It was a great surprise to Our Town when Judge
Juggins' wife, Mrs. Juggins, sued him for divorce,
charging him with extreme cruelty.

She said he was in the habit of giving her a sound
thrashing on an average of once a week. She said he
always used a buggy whip on her, and that he had
worn out 118 buggy whips in the thirty-two years
that they were married.

Judge Juggins was coming up for re-election at the
time. He had then been on the bench of the District
Court for twenty-four years.

The suit created a sensation.

Everybody talked it over at great length.

Then everybody decided that Judge Juggins was
such a just man that he would not have thrashed his
wife with a buggy whip unless she needed thrashing.

So Judge Juggins was re-elected by a large plu-
rality.

The first case that came before Judge Juggins after
his election was that of Hiram Hobarth, who was
arrested for beating his wife with his fists, and Judge
Juggins gave him a year in the county jail.

That is how just Judge Juggins was.

Banker Beaverbrook

Banker Beaverbrook was very rich. He was president of the Cattle Growers' Bank.

He was head of most of our public utilities.

He was about sixty-two years old, and good-looking, except for a big wen on his forehead.

Banker Beaverbrook had a wife, who hated him, and three daughters and two sons, all grown.

They did not care much about him either, because Banker Beaverbrook was a man of simple tastes, who liked quiet, while his wife and children were very social, and always on the go.

They loved to make a big show of themselves.

Banker Beaverbrook had been a laborer in his youth, and he had worked hard all his life. His wife, who hated him, had been the daughter of one of our first families, and she never got over thinking she was much better than Banker Beaverbrook. She was a very haughty old gal.

Banker Beaverbrook's sons and daughters were haughty, too.

So when Banker Beaverbrook wanted a little peace and quiet he used to go to the modest cottage of Miss

Mary Simkins, at the foot of Rambold Street, which is not a very select neighborhood.

Miss Mary Simkins was a milliner.

Banker Beaverbrook had met her when she was 23, and very nice-looking, and he had been going to her cottage for peace and quiet for twenty years. Many people in Our Town knew this, but they thought perhaps Banker Beaverbrook went there because Miss Mary Simkins could cook baked beans very nicely.

Banker Beaverbrook loved baked beans.

He could not get them in his own home.

Miss Mary Simkins never married, though for a while she had many chances, because she knew Banker Beaverbrook would not enjoy a husband around her cottage. She was very fond of Banker Beaverbrook and read books to him, and rubbed his forehead with her hand when he had a headache.

One morning, Banker Beaverbrook was found dead in his bed at home. His will read:

I leave all to my beloved wife.

Miss Mary Simkins was evicted from her cottage by the administrators of Banker Beaverbrook's estate a short time after his death, because she did not have money enough to pay the rent.

Judge Joes

Judge Joes was seventy-five years old.

He had seven of his own teeth.

He could hear good, too, unless you asked him for money.

He had $8,ooo cash in the bank.

He had a little arthritis in his knees, but it only bothered him when the weather got cold.

Judge Joes was highly respected in Our Town. He had held many offices of public trust. He had been married a couple of times, and had grown sons and daughters, and a few grandchildren here and there.

They all raised a terrible row when Judge Joes decided to get married again, especially when he picked out Miss Anastacia Club, who was only twenty-seven. She was a nice girl.

She had been Judge Joes' secretary for some years.

When Judge Joes announced that he was going to marry Miss Anastacia Club, everybody said they had suspected them for a long time.

Judge Joes' children and grandchildren said he must be crazy.

They talked of putting him away.

Other people said he was a nincompoop.

Miss Anastacia Club said the reason she was marrying was because she loved and respected him.

Everybody in Our Town laughed.

Everybody said Miss Anastacia Club must be after his money.

But Judge Joes and Miss Anastacia Club went ahead and got married just the same, and Judge Joes announced that he was giving all his money to his children and grandchildren immediately, so they all attended the wedding and wished them many happy returns.

None of them meant it.

It was a nice occasion, and everything went off well, except that Judge Joes forgot to bring his upper plate, and his answers to the minister could hardly be understood.

Judge Joes' children and grandchildren were pretty hot when it came out afterwards that Miss Anastacia Club had money of her own that had been left to her.

They talked of suing her.

The marriage turned out a happy one, but it caused a lot of trouble.

For the next two years, the young gals in Our Town couldn't go along the street without a bodyguard because of the old plugs from sixty years and up trying to flirt.

Angel Kake

Angel Kake was no angel.

He was a real estate man.

His name was Severance Kake, but he was called Angel for a nickname.

Angel Kake had a picture of Abraham Lincoln hanging on the wall of his office.

Very few people in Our Town trusted Angel Kake.

Angel Kake was thirty-six years old, and was engaged to marry Miss Blanche Astee, who was a telephone operator in the main office of the telephone company. They had been engaged about six years, and Miss Blanche Astee had gotten around to where she was thirty-two years old, and was asking Kake questions.

She was a nice looking girl, but she never bobbed her hair.

She was the only female in Our Town who wore a petticoat. Angel Kake used to always be making excuses for not taking her out.

He was doing very well in the real estate business. He bought and sold property for himself, and for others, and rented houses, and was third vice president of the Chamber of Commerce.

He hoped to be president of the Chamber of Commerce some day. Angel Kake was very ambitious.

One day a young fellow by the name of Erasmus Bidge came to Our Town from Chicago. He said he had been in the oil business in Texas, but was looking for a job. He got acquainted with Angel Kake, and used to drive around with him when Angel Kake was selling real estate.

Erasmus Bidge was with Angel Kake the day Angel took a man from Omaha named Mr. Trumbull out to see the Kake place north of Our Town.

Mr. Trumbull was looking for a farm, but he saw right away what it took Angel Kake thirty years to find out, that you couldn't even raise hell on the place.

Erasmus Bidge was introduced to Miss Blanche Astee by Angel Kake, and Angel would get Erasmus Bidge to take Miss Blanche Astee out when he had business elsewhere. Angel Kake always had business elsewhere, but he would stake Erasmus Bidge to entertain Miss Blanche Astee at the movies, and buy her a chocolate sundae afterwards. Miss Blanche Astee loved chocolate sundaes.

One day Miss Blanche Astee asked Angel Kake right out about marrying her, and he hemmed and hawed, and said well you see, until she told him she could see what he meant, but that if he didn't want a breach of promise action, he had better make some settlement with her, because she had fooled her best years away with him and look at her now.

For a girl who continued to wear a petticoat, Miss Blanche Astee got very tough about it.

Angel Kake said he didn't have much of anything to make a settlement with and she said he had the old Kake place, and she would take that, as it might make a home for her in her old age.

Angel Kake said he was tickled silly to think he was going to get rid of the old Kake place and Miss Blanche Astee at the same time. He could hardly wait to get to his office.

So Angel Kake deeded the place over to her for one dollar and other valuable considerations, and three days later she married Erasmus Bidge, and six months later they struck oil out there.

Angel Kake sued Mr. and Mrs. Bidge, claiming it was a put-up job, but the case was thrown out of court, and everybody in Our Town laughed at Angel Kake.

He still hopes to be president of the Chamber of Commerce.

Bet Ragle

Bet Ragle was very eccentric.

His full name was Bettinger Ragle. He was called Bet for short.

He was an upholsterer.

He wore round, detachable cuffs, and never had much to say.

They were the last round, detachable cuffs in our section of the country.

One day Bet Ragle killed Slogan Carstairs by hitting him on the head with a coupling pin. Bet Ragle used the coupling pin to prop up a window in his upholstering shop.

Slogan Carstairs was walking past the shop, and Bet Ragle took the coupling pin from under the window and said, Hello, Slogan, and then biffed Slogan Carstairs on the conk with the pin.

Slogan Carstairs passed away immediately.

The window dropped down without the coupling pin under it, and it cost Bet Ragle $1.25 to repair the broken panes afterwards.

Slogan Carstairs was one of the worst men in Our Town. He would have been the worst but for J. A. T. Huber, and three men on the South Side.

Slogan Carstairs lied and cheated all his life. He was always drunk. He beat his wife. He starved his children. He was a draft dodger during the war. He was a bootlegger during Prohibition. He was a scab in the steelworkers' strike. He was once convicted of arson. He was suspected of criminal assault.

Slogan Carstairs was really an undesirable citizen.

Bet Ragle was arrested for killing Slogan Carstairs, and caused great surprise in Our Town by stating that he barely knew the deceased, and that he had no grudge against the deceased on any account whatever.

Bet Ragle said he had merely heard everybody in Our Town saying for twenty years that Slogan Carstairs ought to be killed, and that when a chance to kill Slogan Carstairs came his way, he decided that he might as well do what everybody agreed ought to be done. He said it was no bother to him at all.

This statement caused great confusion.

The authorities in Our Town scarcely knew what to do about it.

They agreed that Bet Ragle was quite right, but they did not feel that they could dismiss the matter without some action.

So Bet Ragle was declared temporarily insane, and was locked up in the State asylum for three months. Bet Ragle did not mind so much, but they made him upholster all the worn-out furniture in the asylum and didn't pay him a dime for the job.

Bet Ragle has been talking of moving to some more grateful community ever since, and most people in Our Town agree that he is absolutely right.

Hank Smith

In Our Town lives a great American patriot. Let us have this one with incidental music.

O Columbia the Gem of the Ocean!

His name is Hank Smith. He is sixty years old, unmarried, and very cranky. He was born in Atlanta, Georgia.

Does the Sun Really Shine All the Time?

In 1898 Hank Smith enlisted in the United States Army for the war with Spain. He was twice wounded in that war. The first time was in the old Thalia Café on the Barbary Coast in San Francisco. A lady hit him on the head with a bottle containing beer. She inflicted a severe scalp wound on Hank. It was Budweiser beer. She had little provocation.

When I First Met Kate By the Golden Gate.

Hank fought 'neath the Stars and Stripes at the fall of Manila and was wounded the second time in the Sampoloc district of that city when a Mestizo lady for whom his love had grown cold struck him with a kris. She missed his liver an inch. The kris had a lovely handle.

But My Heart Belongs to Daddy.

Hank fought through the Filipino Insurrection and

was wounded in that, too. An American nurse from Iowa jabbed him in the right hip with a knitting needle with which she was knitting abdominal bandages for the brave soldiers. Hank was only trying to teach her some new wrestling holds. The abdominal bandages made excellent gun wipers for the brave soldiers.

O There's One Red Rose the Soldier Knows.

Hank's regiment was sent to China and Hank fought in the Boxer uprising and was again wounded. In the City of Pekin, a Chinese lady whose love for Hank grew cold, struck him on the left ear with a jade jar that Hank had looted from the residence of a local mandarin. She gave him a cauliflower ear. It was a mighty pretty jar.

Chinatown, My Chinatown.

In 1916 Hank was a civilian scout with General Pershing's expeditionary forces in pursuit of Villa in Mexico. At Casa Grande, in the State of Chihuahua, a Mexican lady by the name of Mercedes to whom Hank had said hello a few times, shot off the lower lobe of his right ear with a .38-calibre pistol. That gave Hank two bum ears. It was a pearl-handled pistol.

Mexicali Rose, Good-bye.

In 1917, Hank got back in the army and went to France. He fought at Château Thierry and was wounded in Paris by a French lady who misunder-

stood his French. She slid a chair in his path when
he tried to get closer to her to make himself clearer
and he fell over the obstacle and sprained his ankle.
It was a Louis XVI chair.

How You Gonna Keep 'Em Down on the Farm?

He battled with his command through the Ar-
gonne and was wounded at Bar-le-Duc by a waitress
in the Hotel Commerce who did not understand his
French and broke his nose with a bowl of soup. It
was good vegetable soup. She threw a curve at Hank
with it.

Madelon, Madelon, Madelon!

His regiment was assigned to the Army of Occu-
pation and at Coblenz on the Rhine Hank was
wounded once more. A German lady dropped a
flowerpot on his head from two stories up. Hank
had knocked at her door to inquire his way. He
wanted to know his way up there. The flowers were
geraniums.

In the Morn I Bring Thee Violets.

He was mighty glad when he got back to his home
up our street and was able to settle down to a life
of peace and quiet. He said he was commencing to
feel the consequences of the many wounds he had in-
curred fighting under the Stars and Stripes, but he
said he would stand ready to answer his country's call
as long as he could totter.

Franklin D. Roosevelt Jones.

The last time Hank ever wore his uniform was when the American Legion held its convention in New York City and they brought him home in an ambulance suffering many bruises and contusions. He had been in the Battle of Times Square and a lady from Idaho had mistaken his friendly spirit and had tripped him up and walked back and forth on him in her high-heeled shoes. Hank says it reminded him of old times when he was a working patriot.

Thanks for the Memory.